The Emperor's New Clothes

and other stories

First published in 2001 by Miles Kelly Publishing,
Bardfield Centre, Great Bardfield, Essex CM7 4SL

Printed in China

Copyright © Miles Kelly Publishing Ltd 2001

Project manager: Paula Borton
Editorial Assistant: Isla MacCuish

British Library Cataloguing-in-Publication Data
A catalogue record for this book is available from the British Library

ISBN 1-84236-049-3

24681097531

Visit us on the web:
www.mileskelly.net
Info@mileskelly.net

The Emperor's New Clothes
and other stories

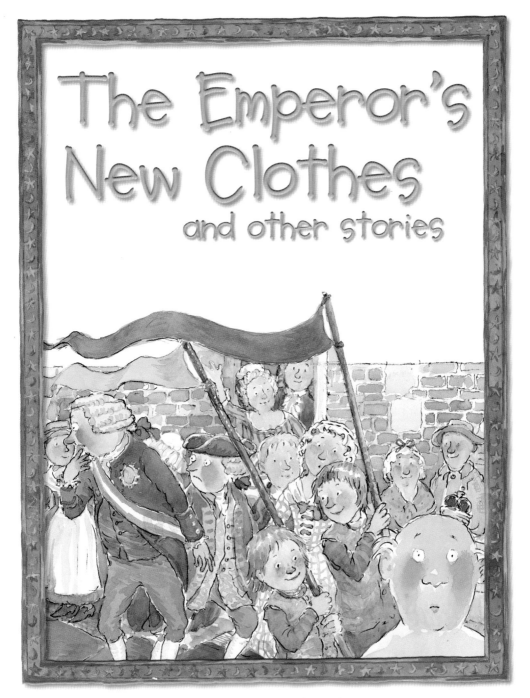

Edited by Vic Parker

Miles Kelly
PUBLISHING

Contents

THE POT OF GOLD

an Irish folk tale

Niall O'Leary was sitting on a gate in the sunshine, daydreaming quite happily, when – TIC! TIC! TIC! – he became aware of a sharp sound coming from the field behind him.

"Now what on earth can that be?" Niall wondered to himself. "It's too loud to be a grasshopper . . . and it's too quiet to be a bird."

TIC! TIC! TIC! it went.

Niall O'Leary swung his legs over the gate and turned around. He blinked in astonishment. There in the long grass of the field was the tiniest man Niall had ever seen, no higher than his boot. The tiny man had his back to Niall, but Niall could see that he was dressed all in green, with a long white feather in his cap. A tiny leather shoe lay before him on a rock, and he was banging away at it with a tiny stone hammer.

Niall's eyes lit up. A leprechaun! A real, live leprechaun! Niall licked his lips greedily.

Every tiny leprechaun had a huge pot of gold hidden somewhere.
And as everybody knew, if you caught hold of a leprechaun and
squeezed him tightly enough, he would have to tell you where his
treasure was buried.

Quietly, quietly, Niall O'Leary got down from the gate.

TIC! TIC! TIC! went the leprechaun's hammer.

Quietly, quietly, Niall O'Leary crept through the grass.

TIC! TIC! TIC! went the leprechaun's hammer.

Quietly, quietly, Niall O'Leary reached out with his large,
meaty hands . . .

"GOTCHA!" cried Niall O'Leary, and he squeezed and
squeezed the wriggling leprechaun with all his might.

"Ooooof!" cried the leprechaun. "Let me go, you big bully!"

"Tell me where your gold is and I will!" boomed Niall.

"I can't tell you anything while you're squeezing the breath out
of me," the leprechaun gasped, looking rather purple.

"Oops, sorry!" blustered Niall, and he relaxed his grip a little.

"That's better," wheezed the
leprechaun, taking big gulps of air. "Now
put me down and I promise I'll show
you where my gold is hidden."

A broad grin spread across Niall's
face as he lowered the leprechaun
back down to the grass. "A
leprechaun can't break his promise!"
he chuckled.

"No," grumbled the leprechaun rather crossly, "and my gold is
buried under here." He leapt a few steps into the middle of the field
and pointed at a clump of dandelions. "You'll need a spade, mind,"

the leprechaun added thoughtfully. "You'll have to dig quite a way down."

Niall's face fell. "But I haven't got a spade with me," he said, glumly. "What shall I do?"

"Why don't you tie your handkerchief around the dandelions so you don't forget where the gold is buried," the leprechaun suggested. "Then hurry back home and fetch a spade. I promise on my word of honour that I won't untie the handkerchief."

Niall's face brightened once again. "What a great idea!" he beamed. He fumbled in his pocket, brought out a rather grubby red silk handkerchief, and tied it around the clump of dandelions. It waved at him in the breeze like a cheerful flag. "Thank you Mr Leprechaun," Niall remembered to say politely. "You've been mighty helpful." Then in a few strides, he was back over the gate and away home, humming merrily.

As soon as Niall had grabbed the biggest spade he could find in the garden shed, he set off back to the field at once. All the way down the lane, he day-dreamed of what he would do with the gold. But when Niall O'Leary reached the gate, he stopped stone-still and his mouth hung open. He dropped the spade and scratched his head. "Well, blow me down," gasped Niall. All over the field, thousands of red silk handkerchiefs were tied onto clumps of dandelions and fluttering in the breeze. And Niall could hear the sound of gleeful leprechaun laughter floating over the grass on the wind.

So Niall O'Leary never got his pot of gold after all. But that is how he came to own the most successful silk handkerchief shop in the whole of Ireland . . .

THE WILD SWANS

a retelling from the original story by Hans Christian Andersen

A long time ago, in a land far away, there lived a king whose wife died, leaving him with eleven little sons and a baby daughter, Elise. The king married again and the children's new stepmother was cruel and jealous. She seemed to put the king under a wicked spell which made him forget all about his beloved children. So the queen sent little Elise away from the palace to be brought up by a peasant couple who lived in the forest. Then she used witchcraft to turn the princes into swans and she sent them flying off from the palace forever.

Many years passed and Elise thought she would never see her brothers again. Then one evening, as she was sitting by a lake watching the sun set, she saw a line of swans come flying like a white ribbon across the sky. They alighted next to her, and at the exact moment when the sun melted into the lake, the swans disappeared in a flutter of feathers. In their place stood eleven princes. They were Elise's long-lost brothers! They recognised each other at once, and they ran to hug each other, weeping tears of joy.

"We have to live as swans by day," the princes explained, "but at night we return to our true selves. Our wicked stepmother banished us to live in a country which lies across a wide sea and we are only allowed to return here once a year for just eleven days. Tomorrow is the day that we must leave once again. Little sister, it is a dangerous journey, but now we have found you, we will take you with us."

All night long, the princes gathered willow bark and tough reeds and rushes and Elise wove them into a strong net. By sunrise, as the princes fluttered back into swans, Elise was lying in the woven mesh, fast asleep. The swans seized the net strings and, with a few powerful wingbeats, sped off into the sky. And so the brothers carried their sister, right across the land and over the churning sea . . .

High above the waves, Elise dreamed she saw a beautiful fairy who smiled sadly and said, "If you are very brave, you can set your brothers free from their enchantment. You must go to the churchyard and pick the stinging nettles that grow on the graves there. They will burn and blister your skin, but you must pick them with your bare hands and then crush them with your bare feet. Twine the nettles into flax and weave eleven shirts with long sleeves. The second that you throw the shirts over your brothers, they will be swans no longer. But mark this well, from the moment you start your task, you must not speak. If you utter a single word, it will be like a dagger through your brothers' hearts and they will surely die."

Elise awoke with a start to find herself lying on a bed of moss in a great cavern, shaded with vines and creepers. Her brothers were flown, and strangely there was a stinging nettle lying next to her. At once, she slipped away to find the churchyard. The graves were silent and spooky, but Elise clambered all over them collecting the nettles that sprang there in thick clumps. How the nettles burnt and blistered her hands! Elise hurried back to the cave and trampled on the nettles until they were crushed and her feet swollen and sore. Finally, she twisted the stalks into flax and began carefully to weave . . .

Elise's work was clumsy and slow due to her red, painful hands and arms. But by the evening when the swans returned, she had woven nearly half of the first shirt. The princes were upset by Elise's strange task and scared by her silence. But when they saw the spark of hope in Elise's eyes, they realised that she must be suffering for their sake. The youngest brother wept for his sister's pain, and as his tears fell onto her injured arms and hands, the blisters healed themselves and disappeared.

Elise would have worked around the clock, until all eleven shirts were finished and the spell finally broken. However, the next day, her hiding place in the cavern was sniffed out by hunting dogs and a royal hunting party burst in upon her. Elise was terrified, but she knew that if she uttered a single word, her brothers would die. The king thought that Elise was the most beautiful girl he had ever seen. "Don't be afraid," he said gently to her, as she stood trembling and silent. "Whoever you are, you can't live here in this cave. You will come back to my palace and I will make sure you are looked after and taken care of." The king lifted Elise up behind him

on his horse and they were off like the wind over the hills.

Elise wept without a word as the ladies of the court dressed her in silks and satins, threaded pearls in her hair, and led her into a splendid banquet which the king had ordered in her honour. "You will be my queen," the king told Elise gently after the feast, "but I do not want you to be sad. I want you to be happy here with me." The king led Elise down a corridor to a small door. He opened it and Elise's mouth widened into a perfect "O" of surprise. The room was adorned with green hangings, to look just like the cave in the forest. And on the floor was the shirt she had finished and all the bundles of nettles from the churchyard. Elise flung her arms around the king and kissed his face and hands as he handed her the key to the little room.

After that, Elise spent every day at the king's side. She could see that he was good and kind and thoughtful, and she longed to tell him how much she had begun to care for him – but she dared not utter a sound. Every night, Elise crept down the corridor in her nightdress to her secret little room and continued with her weaving. Her heart was heavy with the thought that her brothers did not know where she was and must be searching anxiously for her.

Night after night, the pile of flax grew lower and lower, and by the time the tenth shirt was finished, Elise was in desperate need of more nettles. There was nothing for it but to creep out of the palace by moonlight, and hurry down the dark paths all the way to the churchyard. When Elise reached the graves, her blood ran cold with horror. Witches sat on the tombstones, reaching down into the earth with their bony fingers. Elise thought of her brothers and forced herself to walk past the witches and collect huge armfuls of the burning nettles. Then she was away, hurrying back to the palace before dawn . . .

Unbeknown to Elise, the king's chief advisor had spied on her. He had always been jealous of the wild, silent girl from the cave who had won the king's heart and now sat at the king's side instead of him. His wicked heart leapt for joy as he hurried to the king the very next morning. "Your majesty," the chief advisor whispered, "I am sorry to tell you that I saw your bride-to-be at the churchyard last night, surrounded by witches. She can only have been performing black magic."

The king shook his head vigorously. "You must be mistaken," he said. "I do not believe it."

"Go to Elise's room and see the new pile of churchyard nettles she collected for her spells," the chief advisor insisted. "She is a witch and she must be burnt. The people will find out and they will demand it."

The king hung his head in sorrow. He felt as though his heart was breaking.

Next morning, guards broke into Elise's chamber and hauled her away to a dark, damp prison. They left her with only her nettles for a pillow and the shirts she had woven to keep her warm but they were all Elise wanted. Elise didn't know what she had done wrong, but she knew she was going to die and that she didn't have much time left. Her hands trembled as she hurried desperately to finish the final shirt. As she twisted and plaited and wove, a swan came flapping his wings against the window. Elise recognised her youngest brother and she ran to thrust her fingers through the bars and stroke his feathers. She couldn't say a word to tell him what had happened, and tears sparkled in her eyes as she waved him away and hurried back to her work . . .

All day and all night, Elise's sore fingers worked faster than ever. As the sun's rays stretched through the bars, the final shirt was nearly, nearly finished . . . Elise didn't stop frantically working even when the guards thrust her into a smelly cart and they went bumping through the streets. Crowds of people threw mud at her and jeered. "Look at the witch!" they shouted. "See, she's working on some evil spell!"

Then the cart arrived at the bonfire and the executioner stepped forwards to drag Elise to her death. But suddenly, eleven huge white swans swooped down out of the sky. Quick as a flash, Elise grabbed the shirts and threw them over the birds.

The crowd fell back in terror as there was a huge flash of lightning. The swans disappeared and in their places stood eleven handsome princes – although the youngest had a swan's wing instead of one arm, for Elise had run out of time to finish the final sleeve of his shirt.

"Now I can speak!" Elise sobbed. "I am innocent!" She sank into her brothers' arms and the princes explained all that had happened. Then the people began to cheer and the church bells rang out for joy, and the king took his beautiful bride and her brothers back home to his palace.

THE PIED PIPER OF HAMELIN

a German legend

I magine what it would be like to live in a town overrun by rats. Rats in the streets, the shops, the gardens! Rats in the town hall, the hospital and police station! Rats in your school corridors, your classroom, your desk! Rats in your kitchen, your bath, your bed! Well, that's what it was like to live in the town of Hamelin, which lay beside the River Weser.

No one knew where the rats had come from or how they had managed to take over the town in such numbers. The townspeople of Hamelin were desperate to be rid of them. They couldn't eat without rats nibbling off their plates. They couldn't get dressed without uncovering rats nesting in their clothes and boots. They couldn't put their babies down to sleep without finding rats cuddled up in the cradles. They couldn't even chat to each other in comfort, for the noise of all the squeaking and scampering! So you can see why the mayor put up a poster outside the town hall saying:

There will be a reward of
ONE THOUSAND GUILDERS
to anyone who can get rid of the rats!

Yes, one thousand guilders! Everyone began to imagine what they would do with such a huge fortune – but of course, they could only dream. No one had the first idea how to begin claiming their town back from the rats.

By the time the stranger came knocking on the door of the town hall, the mayor was panic-stricken. He would have listened to anybody who said they could help. So when the stranger announced confidently, "I can get rid of all the rats for you," the mayor didn't worry too much about the stranger's odd, multicoloured costume. The mayor paid no attention to the stranger's extraordinarily long fingers and the unusual pipe that hung on a cord round his neck. The mayor didn't think too much about the sad smile on the stranger's face or the wistful gleam in his eyes. The mayor just beamed with relief and said, "GREAT! When can you begin?"

"Right now," replied the stranger, and he raised his pipe to his lips. Off he went, out of the town hall and into the street, playing a lilting tune that filled the air. Instantly, all over town, the rats stopped scuffling, pricked up their ears, and listened. For the first time in many, many months, there was silence for a moment. Then the scampering and squeaking began again, as the rats ran to follow the Pied Piper.

The townspeople of Weser couldn't believe their eyes. All through the town strolled the Pied Piper, his fingers continually moving on his pipe and the haunting notes rippling through the air. And out of all the houses swarmed the rats; out of every garden and gutter, out of every nook and cranny they came streaming. Down stairwells and through streets, out of passages and alleyways, over rooftops and along roads the rats came hurrying after the strange musician. And the Pied Piper didn't stop playing all the way to the wide River Weser. He didn't stop playing as he dipped one brightly coloured foot into the rushing waters and the thousands of rats began to plunge off the bank into the river. He didn't stop playing until the very last rat had drowned.

Then the church bells rang out in celebration, the townspeople started hugging each other, the children began dancing and singing – and the Pied Piper strode quietly back to the town hall to fetch his reward.

"My one thousand guilders, if you please," said the Pied Piper, calmly.

The mayor just smiled what he thought was a charming smile. Now the rats were dead and gone he certainly didn't plan on giving away what was nearly the entire contents of the town council bank account! "Come, come now, my dear fellow," the mayor coaxed. "One thousand guilders is somewhat over-the-top for playing a pretty ditty on a tin whistle, surely you'll agree! Why don't we settle on fifty guilders, and I'll throw in a nice bronze medal and even put up a statue of you and me together in the market place, eh?"

The Pied Piper simply turned on his heel and walked out into the street.

As he went, he once more lifted his pipe to his lips. But this time, he played a different tune. Enchanting notes rippled all around and down the roads the children came dancing, running and leaping after the Pied Piper.

The men and women of Hamelin were struck still with horror as the children swept past them and were gone through the town. Playing his strange melody, the Pied Piper led the children past the River Weser and skipping happily along a path that led up to a steep, craggy mountain. He piped a burst of airy notes and a little door appeared in the mountain slope. The Pied Piper led the children inside. The townspeople could hear the echo of his pipe and the children's laughter grow fainter and fainter as they went deeper and deeper into the earth. Then suddenly, the little door slammed shut and disappeared. The children were gone – all except for one little boy who was lame and so hadn't been able to keep up with the others. He stood on the mountainside and sobbed, calling out for his friends. But the little door had vanished.

No one ever saw the Pied Piper or the children again. But on sunny days, some townsfolk swore they could hear ripples of childish laughter floating down from the mountain. And from that day to this, there has never been a single rat in the town of Hamelin.

BELLE AND THE BEAST

a retelling from the original tale by Madame Leprince de Beaumont

There was once a businessman who had made a fortune by trading overseas. He lived in a magnificent mansion staffed by servants and with a TV in every room – including the indoor swimming pool. The businessman's wife had died, so he had brought up their three beautiful daughters on his own. Unfortunately, the two eldest girls, Bianca and Bettina, lazed about all day watching chat shows, flicking through magazines and day-dreaming of marrying professional footballers. But Belle, the youngest daughter, was a great help to her father in running his business. She also enjoyed reading books on engineering and space exploration, for she was as intelligent as she was beautiful, and she had an avid interest in rocket science.

The businessman once had to go away on an important trip for work.

"Don't forget to bring us back some jewellery!" yelled Bianca.

"And some perfume!" bellowed Bettina.

"Is there nothing you would like, darling?" the businessman asked Belle.

Belle thought for a while. "Just a beautiful rose, please Daddy," she smiled.

"That's my girl!" the businessman said, and gave a cheery wave as he drove away.

But when the businessman finally returned, he was downcast and empty-handed.

"I'm afraid your dear old Dad has had it," the businessman explained. "I was on my way back last night, but it was dark and raining and somehow I got completely lost in the middle of nowhere. The only house for miles around was a spooky old mansion, and I went to ask for help. The lights were on, the front door was open, but nobody seemed to be at home. I thought it was very strange, but I was so desperate that I crept inside and stayed the night. Early this morning, as I was hurrying off through the grounds, I stopped to pick a rose for Belle. 'STOP THIEF!' someone roared. 'This is my house and those are my roses! Is this how you repay my hospitality? I am going to kill you!' The man who came striding towards me was uglier than a monster in a film. He had a hairy face and bloodshot eyes, a snout for a nose and teeth like fangs. His hands were clawed and his body huge and hulking. I realised that the beast was deadly serious, so I fell on my knees in terror and begged for mercy. 'I will give you three months to say goodbye to everyone,' he growled. 'After that, you must return here to die . . . unless you have a daughter who is willing to come in your place and live here with me forever.'"

Bianca and Bettina stood gawping in horror. "Oh Daddy," they wailed, "who is going to look after us when you're gone?"

"Don't worry, Daddy," Belle comforted her father. "I can't let you die. I will go instead of you."

"Belle, you will do nothing of the kind!" her father protested. "You haven't seen this guy!"

"I don't care!" said Belle, resolutely sticking out her chin. And nothing Belle's father could say would make her change her mind. "If you sneak off without me, I shall just follow you," was her final word on the subject. So three months later, the broken-hearted businessman accompanied his brave daughter to the door of the huge, lonely mansion and kissed her for the last time. He could hardly see through his tears as he turned and walked away . . .

"Right," Belle said to herself firmly, though her bottom lip was trembling. "Let's find the library. Maybe it has a good science section." She set off through the stone corridors and oak-panelled halls, exploring. It was an eerie feeling to be all alone in such an enormous old place. Suddenly, Belle stopped in surprise. There, right in front of her was a door marked 'Belle's room'. She put her hand on the iron handle and gently pushed. It swung open with a creak. Belle gasped with delight. Inside, was everything she could possibly have wished for. There was a soft, white bed. Wardrobes full of beautiful clothes. But best of all, lining the walls was shelf after shelf of books.

"The owner of this place can't be all bad," Belle murmured to herself. She drew down the nearest book. It was bound in ancient leather and had gold-edging. She read the first page:

Belle, you have a heart of gold
Like girls in fairytales of old.
Whatever you wish, it will come true
There's magic waiting here for you.

"Hmmm," wondered Belle. "Well, the only thing I really wish is that I could see if my Dad is okay."

At that very moment, Belle noticed a mirror on the bedroom wall begin to cloud over. Mists swirled across the glass, and when they cleared, instead of her own reflection, she saw a picture of her father, sitting at home sadly without her. After a few moments the picture vanished, but Belle was very grateful to have been able to see her father at all. *The owner of this place is actually very kind,* Belle thought to herself.

Just then, Belle heard the dinner bell ringing from the great hall. She hurried along and found a delicious meal laid out for one. No sooner had she swallowed three mouthfuls than she heard a shuffling and a snuffling. The food stuck in her throat and her heartbeat quickened. Belle forced herself to turn round and face her host.

Her father had been right. He was truly hideous.

"I'm Belle," she whispered, remembering her manners, like the well-brought up girl she was. "My room is wonderful – thank you."

"Call me Beast," said the monster gruffly, a look of pleasure lighting up his sad eyes. "Did you really like everything?"

"Yes, of course," said Belle. "Particularly the books. I love books, especially those on rocket science."

"They are your books now," said Beast. "Everything here is yours. I give it all to you. You can do with everything just what you wish. That goes for me, too. If I'm bothering you just tell me to go away and I will." The Beast looked down at his huge, flat feet. "I know I'm exceedingly ugly. I might put you off your food." He sighed a deep sigh. "And not only am I ugly, I'm very stupid too."

"Now, now," comforted Belle. "I'm sure that's not the case. Anyone who is ready to say they are stupid can't possibly be stupid. The only people who really are stupid are those who won't admit that they're stupid!"

"Do you really think so?" sighed the Beast.

"Yes, of course!" laughed Belle. "And if you're really worried about being stupid, I can teach you all about rocket science. Let me get my books . . ."

A sheepish smile came over the Beast's ugly face as he listened to Belle read. After a while, he suddenly interrupted her.

"Belle, will you marry me?" he asked.

Belle was extremely taken aback. She looked at the monster as he crouched adoringly in front of her. "I'm sorry," she said. "I wish I could, but I really don't want to."

And so the time passed. Each day, Belle read in her room and walked in the beautiful grounds, admiring the roses. And each evening, the Beast came to visit her. As the weeks went on, Belle began to enjoy his company and looked forward to seeing him. But each night the Beast asked her to marry him, and even though Belle liked him more and more as a friend, she simply couldn't – well, *fancy* him.

Belle's only other worry was her Dad. Each day she saw in the mirror that he was pining more and more without her. Her sisters were selfish, unkind and thoughtless, and her father had grown quiet and pale and thin.

"Dear Beast," Belle begged one night, "allow me to go back to see my dad. I am afraid that he is dying of a broken heart."

Much to Belle's surprise, the Beast nodded his agreement. "Of course, Belle," he said, "if that is what will make you happy. Only I don't know what I'll do without you . . ."

"Darling Beast," whispered Belle, stroking his matted, shaggy hair, "I promise I'll be back in a week."

"Then I promise you that when you wake up tomorrow morning, you'll be at home with your father," sighed the Beast. "Take this ring. When you're ready to leave, just put it by the side of your bed at night. As you sleep, it will bring you back here."

Sure enough, next morning Belle woke up back in her old bed. Her dad couldn't believe his eyes! He and Belle hugged and laughed and spent a wonderful holiday doing all the things they used to enjoy doing together – going through his accounts, visiting the science museum, watching old musicals on TV . . . The week flew by in the twinkling of an eye. "Please, Belle, don't go," begged her dad, and Belle didn't have the heart to leave.

But several nights later, Belle had a terrible dream. She saw the Beast lying in the garden of his mansion, under the rose bushes that he loved so much. Belle knew that he was dying. "Daddy," she sobbed the next morning. "I'm worried that something dreadful has happened to the Beast. He's my best and truest friend – and it's all my fault!"

That night, Belle put the Beast's ring by her bedside. It didn't seem as if she'd been asleep for five minutes when she woke up in her beautiful white room in the mansion. Belle sped off into the moonlit garden and there, lying under the rose bushes just as in her dream, lay the Beast. She flung herself down by his side and heaved his big, heavy head into her lap. Her tears plopped one by one onto his hairy face.

Weakly, the Beast opened his eyes and smiled. "I thought you had forgotten your promise," he whispered. "Now I have seen you once again, I can die happily."

"No!" Belle cried. "You can't die! You mustn't leave me! I love you!" And she kissed him.

At that very moment, the night sky was lit up by a million rainbow-coloured fireworks. Belle gazed upwards in surprise – she thought things like that only happened in films. When she looked back down at the Beast again, the monster was gone. Lying in her lap was a handsome, happy prince. He sprang up and lifted Belle to her feet with joy in his eyes.

"My darling Belle," he told her, "Thank you for setting me free! I have lived under a wicked enchantment for years which forced me to appear as the Beast – not only ugly but stupid, too – until a beautiful girl willingly fell in love with me. You are the only person in the world who saw through my ugly appearance and sensed what I was really like inside. Now we will live together happily forever."

And that's exactly what they did. But this is a real tale, not a fairytale, and real tales don't have entirely happy endings. The prince took Belle to live at his palace – and her dad went to live with them too. But Belle's selfish sisters got what they deserved. They were turned into statues and set at the palace gates until such time as they began to think about other people rather than themselves. As far as I know, they're both there still . . .

PANDORA'S BOX
a Greek myth

When the world was first created, it was a happy place of light and laughter; there was no such thing as sadness or pain. The sun shone every day and the gods came down from heaven to walk and talk with the humans who lived on earth.

One afternoon, a man called Epimetheus and his wife, Pandora, were outside tending their flower garden when they saw the god Mercury approaching. He was bowed down by a dark wooden chest that he was carrying on his shoulders and he looked hot and tired. Pandora rushed to get the worn-out god a cool drink, while Epimetheus helped him lower the chest onto the ground. It was tied shut with golden cords and was carved with strange markings.

"My friends, would you do me a great favour?" sighed Mercury. "It is so hot today and the box is so heavy! May I leave it here while I go on an errand?"

"Of course you can," smiled Epimetheus.

The man and the god heaved the chest indoors.

"Are you sure that no one will find it?" asked Mercury

anxiously. "NO ONE under ANY circumstances must open the box."

"Don't worry," laughed Epimetheus and Pandora, and they waved the god off through the trees.

All of a sudden, Pandora stopped still and frowned. "Listen, Epimetheus!" she hissed. "I am sure I heard someone whispering our names!"

Epimetheus and Pandora listened hard. At first, they heard nothing but the twittering of the birds in the sunshine and the rustling of the leaves in the breeze. Then, they heard the distant sound of "Epimetheus! Pandora!" being called from outside.

"It's our friends!" cried Epimetheus, happily.

But Pandora looked puzzled and shook her head. "No, Epimetheus, those aren't the voices I heard," she said, firmly.

"They must have been!" Epimetheus laughed. "Come on now, let's go and see everyone." `

"You go," Pandora insisted, with a frown. "I'd rather stay here for a while."

Epimetheus shrugged, kissed Pandora on the nose, and strode outside. As soon as he was gone,

Pandora hurried over to the strange box and waited. After only a few seconds, she heard it again – distant voices calling "Pandora! Pandora!" The voices were so low and whispery that Pandora wasn't sure whether she really was hearing them or was just imagining it.. She bent down closer and put her ear to the lid. No, this time she was sure.The box was calling to her! "Pandora!" the voices pleaded. "Let us out, Pandora! We are trapped in here in the darkness! Please help us to escape!"

Pandora jumped back with a start. Mercury had expressly forbade them or anyone else to open the box . . . and yet the voices sounded so sad and pitiful.

"Pandora!" they came again. "Help us! Help us, we beg you!"

Pandora could stand it no longer. Hurriedly, she knelt down and worked at the tight golden knots. All the time, the whispering and pleading voices filled her ears. At last the knots were undone and the gleaming cords fell away. She took a deep breath and opened the lid.

At once, Pandora realised she had done a terrible thing. The box had been crammed with all the evils in the world – thousands of tiny, brown, moth-like creatures that stung people with their wings and caused hurt and misery wherever they went. Now, thanks to Pandora, the evils were free! They flew up out of the chest in a great swarm and fluttered all over Pandora's skin. For the very first time, Pandora felt pain and regret. She began to wail with despair, and all too late, she slammed the lid back down onto the box.

Outside, Epimetheus heard his wife's cries and came running as fast as he could. The little creatures fluttered to sting and bite him, before speeding off through the window into the world beyond. For the first time ever, Epimetheus began to shout at his wife in anger. Pandora yelled back, and the couple realised in horror that they were arguing.

"Let me out!" interrupted a high voice. Pandora and Epimetheus grabbed onto each other in a panic. The voice was coming from inside the box. "Don't be afraid of me! Let me out and I can help you!" came the voice once more.

"What do you think?" Pandora whispered to Epimetheus, wide-eyed.

"Surely you can't do any more mischief than you already have done," he grumbled. So Pandora shut her eyes and opened Mercury's chest for a second time.

Out of the deep, dark box fluttered a single shining white spirit like a butterfly. It was Hope. Pandora and Epimetheus sobbed with relief as she fluttered against their skin and soothed their stinging wounds. Then she was gone, darting out of the window and into the world after the evils. And luckily, Hope has stayed with us ever since.

TOMLIN

a Scottish folk tale

Carterhaugh Wood was thick and green and dark, and people said it was the home of fairy folk. One bright summer's day, Janet, the earl's daughter, made up her mind to go and explore it for herself. She crept out of the castle and set off down a narrow path deep into the woods. After a while, Janet reached a small stone well in the middle of a clearing. There were roses climbing all over it – far more beautiful than any in the castle gardens – and Janet bent to pick one. No sooner had the stem broken off in her hand than Janet heard a voice that said, "Naughty-naughty, Janet. Who said you could come here into our wood and pick one of our roses?"

Janet straightened up with a start. There before her stood the most handsome young knight she had ever seen. She tossed her hair proudly and replied, "How dare you speak to me like that! These woods belong to my father, the earl. I shall go where I choose and pick whatever flowers I like!"

Delight sparkled in the young man's eyes at her bold answer and he threw back his head and laughed. "I am Tomlin," the knight said, taking Janet's hands and spinning her round, "and today you shall stay here in the forest with me and we shall play."

All day long, Tomlin and Janet wandered through Carterhaugh Wood. They danced and sang and told each other stories. And by the evening, they were both deeply in love.

"I will not return to the castle without you," Janet vowed. "You must come with me and I will beg my father to let you stay."

"I cannot leave the wood," replied Tomlin sadly. "I was once human, but many years ago, when I was riding through the forest, the Fairy Queen caught me and enchanted me. Now I am an elf-knight, and I must ride by the side of the Fairy Queen to protect her for ever more. I only wish that I could be a man again, for then I would surely marry you."

"Is there no way to break the spell?" Janet sighed.

"There is," Tomlin said gently, "but you must be very brave."

"Tell me what I must do," Janet whispered.

"This very night is Halloween," Tomlin explained, "a night when fairies, goblins and witches ride abroad. You must go to Mile Cross and hide there until midnight, for then I will come riding by. First you will see a troop of riders on black horses. Then there will be a troop on brown horses. Next will come riders on horses as white as milk – and in the middle of them will ride the Fairy Queen herself. I will be among the elf-knights at her side, and I will wear only one glove so you can find me quickly among the throng. When you see me, you must run to my horse, seize its bridle and drag me down. You must then hold me fast, no matter what happens – for the fairy folk will cast all sorts of spells on me to try to keep me. If you have the strength and courage not to let go, the enchantment will at last be broken and I will be yours." Tomlin took Janet's hand. "Do you think you can do all this?" he asked quietly.

"Yes," breathed Janet. "Yes, I will."

Later that night, when everyone else was safely inside the castle with the doors and windows barred, Janet hid in the darkness on the moor at Mile Cross. Just before the stroke of midnight, she heard the thunder of hooves and out of the night appeared hundreds of black horses, bridles jangling and manes flying. On their backs were witches with bony fingers and sunken faces with dead, staring eyes.

Next, the brown horses galloped past, whinnying and snorting. The wrinkled goblins who rode them whipped them with willow switches and clutched the reins with wizened fingers.

Then the white horses came like glowing ghosts through the gloom, wild-eyed and foaming at the mouth, and at the centre of the riders Janet saw the beautiful Fairy Queen, sitting tall and fierce and proud. Quickly, Janet searched for a rider with only one glove. She plunged in among the pounding hooves, pulled down the enchanted elf-knight and held Tomlin to herself as tight as she could.

The Fairy Queen sent up an unearthly wail that tore through the darkness and all the hundreds of riders thundered around, shrieking and howling. Suddenly Janet felt Tomlin grow in her arms and she realised she was holding a huge, hairy bear. Still she held him fast, and he writhed into a hissing snake. Still she clutched him in her arms, and he bucked into an angry, snapping wolf. Still she held on tight, and he turned into a blazing branch that burnt into her flesh. Still Janet refused to let go, and in a flash of cold lightning she saw she was at last holding a naked, human man. As she wrapped Tomlin in her cloak, a haunting cry came from the Fairy Queen: "Tomlin, I would rather have changed your eyes to wood and your heart to stone than lost you!" Then suddenly the wild hunt was gone, disappeared into the night, and Janet and Tomlin were left alone on the dark, windy moor to make their way home to the castle together.

THE EMPEROR'S NEW CLOTHES

retold from the original tale by Hans Christian Andersen

There was once an emperor who loved new clothes above everything else. Designers, tailors, clothmakers, dyers, and specialists in all sorts of needlework travelled to his city from all over the world. Anyone who could suggest flashy, fancy new outfits for the emperor was always very welcome at the palace.

One day, it was the turn of two weavers to be ushered into the emperor's dressing room. The emperor, his butler and all his Officers of the Royal Wardrobe, gasped with amazement as they listened to them describe their work. "We have created a special type of fabric that is so light and airy the wearer cannot feel it is there," the first weaver announced.

"Our samples are top secret, which is why we have not been able to bring any to show you," the second weaver explained.

"However we can assure you that not only are our designs and patterns exquisitely beautiful," said the first weaver, "but the fabric has the unique advantage that it is completely invisible to anyone who is not worthy of his job –"

"– or who is just plain stupid!" laughed the second weaver, and the emperor and all his courtiers gasped and chuckled along.

"We would be honoured if you would like to order the very first suit of clothes made out of this extraordinary fabric, your imperial majesty," said the first weaver, bowing low.

The emperor clapped his hands with delight. "I'd like to place an order right away!" he commanded, and he gave the two weavers a large sum of money so that they could buy the rare, expensive materials they needed and begin their work without delay.

The weavers set up their looms in the palace studio and got going right away. News of the strange cloth spread round the city like wildfire and soon everyone was talking about it. But the weavers worked behind closed doors and no one got even a glimpse of what they were doing. Still, day and night everyone heard the looms clicking and the shuttles flying, and work on the magical cloth seemed to be progressing well.

As the days went on, the emperor began to feel rather uneasy about seeing the cloth for the first time. *Imagine if I can't see the fabric myself!* he thought to himself. *How dreadfully embarrassing that would be!* The worried emperor decided to send his trusted old butler to see how the weavers were getting on. He was sure that his butler was both fit for his job and very wise, and would be sure to see the wonderful material.

The weavers bowed low and ushered the butler into the studio. But the butler couldn't see anything at all. *Heavens above!* the butler thought to himself. *Those looms look totally bare to me! I must either be a very bad butler, or else I'm an idiot. No one must ever find out* . . . So he praised the material that he could not see, told the king that the

weavers' work was indeed
magnificent, and everyone in
the city heard that the cloth
was truly unbelieveable!

Soon afterwards, the weavers
sent word to the emperor that
they needed more money to buy
essential items for the work. The
emperor had been so delighted with
the butler's report that he sent them
twice as much money as before.

The emperor was more excited
than ever. "I'm going to have the
most amazing suit of clothes in the world!" he
giggled to himself ten times a day.

Eventually, just as the impatient emperor thought he was going
to explode with waiting, the weavers announced their work was
finished. They went to the dressing room to present the material to
the emperor amid fanfares of trumpets. "Is the cloth not beautiful
beyond all imagining?" the weavers sighed.

The emperor smiled a wide smile, trying to hide his horror. All
that the weavers appeared to be holding up before him was thin air.
The emperor's worst fear had come true – to him the cloth was
invisible! *I cannot be thought to be a fool or not worthy to be ruler,* the
despairing emperor thought. So he beamed and leant forwards and
inspected the air. "Wonderful! Splendid! Magnificent!" he cried, and
his butler and all the Officers of the Royal Wardrobe nodded and
cried out compliments. None of them could see anything either, but
they weren't about to risk losing their jobs by admitting it.

So the weavers got out their tape measures and their scissors and they set about cutting the thin air (or so it seemed) into a pattern. All night long they sewed with needles which appeared to have no thread, and in the morning they announced that the emperor's new clothes were ready. "Now if your imperial majesty would care to disrobe, we will dress you in the amazing garments."

The emperor swallowed hard and took off all his clothes. The weavers helped him on with the underpants and trousers and shirt and jacket that he couldn't see. "Aren't they lighter than cobwebs?" they sighed. The emperor spluttered his agreement. He couldn't feel that he had any clothes on at all.

The emperor stood back and looked at himself in the mirror. According to what he saw, he didn't have a stitch on! But he turned this way and that, pretending to admire himself. And the butler and all the Officers of the Royal Wardrobe cried out, "How wonderfully the new clothes fit you, sire!" and "We have never seen the like of the amazing colours!" and "The design is a work of genius!" – even though it looked to them as if the emperor was as naked as the day he was born.

Everyone else can see my new suit except me, the emperor thought to himself glumly. And he walked out of the palace to parade before the people in his marvellous new clothes.

The streets were lined with hundreds of men and women who *ooohed!* and *aaaahed!* over the emperor's invisible new clothes – for none of them wanted to admit that they couldn't see them.

Suddenly, a little boy's shrill voice rose over the applause of the crowd. "But the emperor has nothing on!" the child shouted. "Nothing on at all!" Suddenly there was a stunned silence and the little boy found that hundreds of pairs of eyes were staring at him. Then someone sniggered . . . someone else tried to stifle a giggle . . .

another person guffawed and snorted . . . and the whole crowd burst out into uncontrollable peals of laughter.

The emperor's face turned as red as a ripe tomato. "I am indeed a fool!" he murmured. "I have been swindled by two tricksters!" He ran back to the palace as fast as his short, naked legs could carry him – but the clever (and now very rich) weavers were long gone!

THE LITTLE MERMAID

retold from the original tale by Hans Christian Andersen

Far, far out in the ocean, the water is as blue as cornflowers and deeper than the tallest mountain. It is there that the sea-people live, and in the very deepest waters lies the Sea King's palace of coral and mother-of-pearl. The Sea King's beloved wife had died, so his mother, the old queen, took care of his six beautiful mermaid daughters. All day long, the princesses sang and danced, swimming in and out of the pillars and halls of the palace. Sometimes shy, brightly coloured fish swam up to eat out of their hands. And at other times, each would tend the little garden that she cared for in the royal grounds. Each mermaid princess gave her garden its own particular style and design: one was shaped like a whale; another had a rockery of shells; yet another had flowerbeds where the sea-horses came to graze. But the youngest mermaid's garden was shaped like the sun that shone on the world above the sea, and the flowers that grew there blazed red and orange and yellow like the sunlight.

The little mermaid had never been up to the ocean's surface and seen the upper world, for the princesses were only allowed to do

so when they reached fifteen years
old. But the little mermaid longed
for that day to come. She loved to
hear the stories her grandmother told
of people and ships and cities and
animals and meadows and forests and
the like. And many a night the little
mermaid stood at her open chamber
window, peering up at the watery reflections of
the moon and the stars and the dark shapes of
ships as they passed like clouds above her.

When each of her sisters came of age, the little
mermaid begged them eagerly to tell her everything they
had seen. Then at last, she turned fifteen and it was her turn to see
the upper world for herself.

The little mermaid thought it was more beautiful than she had
ever imagined. Her head broke through the foam when the sun had
just gone down and the clouds looked as if they were on fire with red
and gold. The sound of music and singing was coming from a tall-
masted ship bedecked all about with coloured flags and banners.
Suddenly rockets zoomed up from it into the sky which exploded
into stars that fell glittering all around her – the little mermaid had
never seen fireworks before. When she was lifted up on the swell of
the sea, she saw onto the ship's magnificent deck and understood the
reason for the wonderful celebrations: it was the birthday party of a
prince, more handsome than any merman she had ever seen.

As the little mermaid gazed with delight at the prince and his
ship, she heard a familiar rumbling stirring deep within the sea. A
storm was coming! All at once the sky darkened. Sheets of rain

lashed the ship. The waves towered into mountains that hurled the ship upwards and sent it crashing down towards the depths. The little mermaid saw with alarm that the ship wouldn't be able to hold out against the might of the weather and the ocean, and she ducked under the waves as wooden planks and other pieces of the ship came flying out of the darkness at her head. Through the murky waters, the little mermaid was horrified to see human bodies come floating down around her – and among them was her beautiful prince, choking and gasping for air.

The little mermaid shot through the water and clutched him close to her, and began swimming up to the light until his head was above water. The little mermaid hauled the exhausted prince to the shore and let the waves wash him onto the sand, and she stayed in the foam and watched him until the storm had died away and the morning sunlight came streaming warmly through the clouds. Then she saw the green hills for the first time and heard the peal of bells, and she saw a group of young girls come skipping out of a white building with a cross on the top. One of the girls noticed the prince where he lay. She ran to him and laid his head in her lap, and slowly the prince opened his eyes. He looked up at the girl and smiled, and the little mermaid turned away sadly, for she knew the prince thought it was that girl who had rescued him. Down, down, down, the little mermaid dived into the deeps – and her heart ached all the way back to her father's palace.

From that moment on, the little mermaid was thoughtful and sad. She longed to see her handsome prince again, to tell him that she loved him and wanted to be with him forever. She wanted to be human more than anything else in the whole world. There was only one thing she could do: make the dangerous journey to the cold, dark depths of the ocean to see the Water-Witch.

The Water-Witch's lair was set about with the skeletons of humans she had drowned and the remains of ships she had wrecked. The little mermaid trembled with fear as she explained why she had come.

"What you long for is extremely difficult to give," the Water-Witch cackled. "I can make your tail disappear and give you legs so that you can walk about with the humans in the world above. But every step you take will be as painful as if you are treading on knives. And I cannot make your prince fall in love with you. It is up to you, and you alone, to do that. If your prince marries another, the morning afterwards your heart will break and you will turn to foam on the water."

The little mermaid shuddered, but she bade the Water-Witch continue.

"The price for such strong magic is very high," spat the witch. "Once I have given you legs, there is no changing your mind. You will never be able to return to the sea as a mermaid to see your family . . . And there is one more thing. I cannot mix the potion you need unless you give me your voice."

The little mermaid longed so badly for her prince and for a human soul that she whispered, "So be it." The words were the last sounds she ever uttered. For then the Water-Witch took the little mermaid's voice and brewed up an evil-smelling potion for her in exchange.

The little mermaid felt as if her heart would break with grief as she swam back past her father's palace, leaving her sleeping family for the world above. She splashed onto the sand, half-choking through her tears and half-gasping for air, and looked at her beautiful silvery fishtail for the last time. Then the little mermaid raised the witch's brew to her lips and drank deeply. At once pain wracked her body and she fell into a dead faint . . .

The little mermaid awoke to find her handsome prince standing over her, looking worried. "Are you all right?" he asked, but the little mermaid couldn't reply. Instead, she smiled as she looked down at her body and saw that she had the prettiest pair of legs she could have wished for. Falteringly, she stood up for the very first time. The little mermaid put out her foot – and it was true, each step was like treading on knives. But soon she was dancing and running and skipping along the beach for joy, and the prince was utterly enchanted.

The prince took his new little friend back to the palace and dressed her in fine robes of silk and satin. He didn't seem to mind that she was dumb, and kept her by his side at all times, calling her "my beautiful little foundling".

Yet although the little mermaid was happier than she had ever dreamed was possible, there was a sadness in her eyes and a heaviness in her heart. Each night, she would creep out of the palace and go down to the seashore. Sometimes she saw her sisters way out among the surf, and they would sing to her sadly as they floated on the waves. Once, she even thought she glimpsed the golden crowns of her father and grandmother – but perhaps it was just the moonlight glinting on the water.

Eventually a day came when the
prince led the little mermaid onto a fine
ship just like the one from which she
had rescued him. They sailed for a
night and a day, and all the time the
little mermaid longed to leap into
the waves and dive down to see her
family far below. The ship finally arrived
in the harbour of a neighbouring kingdom,
and all the people lined the streets to meet them,
waving flags and cheering. "See how they welcome me," the prince
whispered to the little mermaid. "For today I am going to marry their
princess."

The little mermaid felt as if someone had grabbed her heart
with icy fingers. Surely it couldn't be true? But when the prince's
bride came running down the palace steps to meet him, the little
mermaid understood. It was the girl who had found him on the
beach; the girl whom the prince thought had saved him from the sea;
the girl whom the prince thought was the little mermaid.

That afternoon, the little mermaid stood in church dressed in
silk and gold, holding the bride's train. And all the way back to the
ship, she cried silent, dry tears.

That night, as the splendid ship floated on the waves, there
were flags and fireworks and music and dancing – and the little
mermaid felt no more a part of the celebrations than she had when
she had watched the prince's birthday party from afar.

The little mermaid stood on the deck all night and listened to
the sighing of the sea. She felt the warm night wind on her face and
her hair floated in the damp sea mists. When the first rays of the

dawn lit up the horizon, the little mermaid prepared herself to dissolve into foam on the waves. But instead, she saw transparent beings of light flying to her through the air. They lifted her up on their wings and soared off into the sky, and the little mermaid found that she was one of them. "We are the daughters of the air," the beautiful beings explained. "We do not have an immortal soul, but if we perform enough acts of goodness and kindness, we will one day win one for ourselves. And this is your reward for the suffering you have endured."

The little mermaid raised her hands towards the sun and the tears in her eyes were tears of joy. She looked down upon the prince and his bride on their ship. They were searching for her sadly in the water, thinking she had fallen overboard. But the little mermaid didn't stay to watch them for long. She blew them a kiss and flew onwards with the daughters of the air.